The Amazing World of
GUMBALL

WHO'D HAVE THUNK IT?

by Wrigley Stuart

PSS!
PRICE STERN SLOAN
AN IMPRINT OF PENGUIN GROUP (USA) LLC

PRICE STERN SLOAN
Published by the Penguin Group
Penguin Group (USA) LLC, 375 Hudson Street,
New York, New York 10014, USA

USA | Canada | UK | Ireland | Australia |
New Zealand | India | South Africa | China

penguin.com
A Penguin Random House Company

Published in 2014 by Price Stern Sloan, a division
of Penguin Young Readers Group, 345 Hudson Street,
New York, New York 10014. *PSS!* is a registered trademark
of Penguin Group (USA) LLC. Printed in the USA.

ISBN 978-0-8431-8106-7   10 9 8 7 6 5 4 3 2 1

I KNOW MORE STUFF THAN YOU.
IMPOSSIBLE. I KNOW EVERYTHING.
DID YOU KNOW THAT I'VE BROKEN 271 BONES? THAT'S MORE BONES THAN IN A CAT'S SKELETON.
OKAY, I DIDN'T KNOW THAT.

If you didn't do your homework, just make sure you have a really good excuse.

MR. WATTERSON CANNOT LAY GOLDEN EGGS. BUT IT'S NOT FOR LACK OF TRYING.

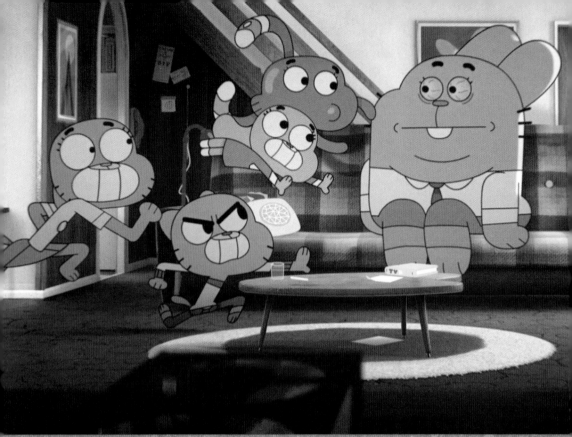

IMPORTANT HOUSEHOLD RULE

Whoever gets the remote first
gets to choose what to watch.

AND PENNY KIND OF LIKES GUMBALL.

GUMBALL SECRETLY LOVES PENNY. WELL, NOT SO SECRETLY.

would you be the Jelly in my peanut butter Sandwich?

Ripley 2000 doesn't accept refunds. But whatever you do, don't mess with the manager.

The problem with having a robot do everything you say is that robots tend to take things literally.

ALAN AND CARMEN
MAKE AN UNLIKELY COUPLE.

THEIR RELATIONSHIP
IS PROBABLY DOOMED.

You shouldn't be angry with your friends
for the things they do in your dreams.
It's not really their fault.

The safe at the gas station will only open if you ask it nicely.

Never mess with a guy holding a spoon.

PENNY LOVES DANCING, CHEERLEADING, AND GUMBALL.

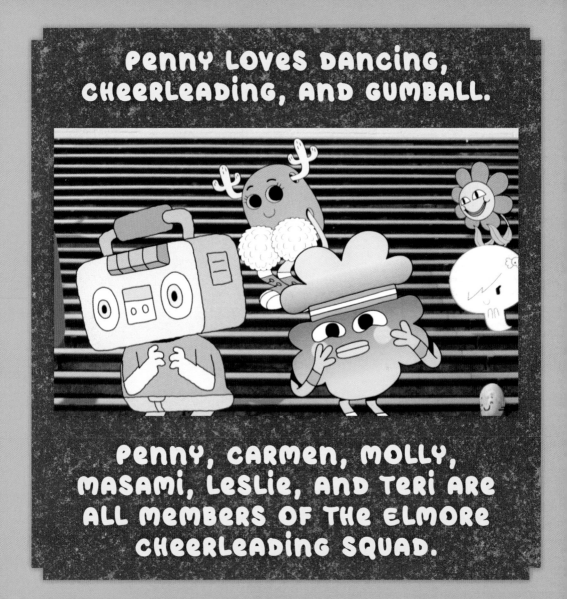

PENNY, CARMEN, MOLLY, MASAMI, LESLIE, AND TERI ARE ALL MEMBERS OF THE ELMORE CHEERLEADING SQUAD.

Paintball can be a very dangerous sport.

THE WATTERSONS' MP3 PLAYER IS JUST A CALCULATOR WITH SOME HEADPHONES STUCK IN IT.

Gumball plays the ukulele, which is a small guitar invented in Hawaii.

ITS NAME ROUGHLY MEANS "JUMPING FLEA."

DARWIN WAS GUMBALL'S PET FISH, UNTIL HE SPROUTED LEGS.

Charles Darwin's theory of evolution suggests that animals change over long periods of time. Like fish growing legs over millions of years (but not overnight).

THE SPACE
BETWEEN OUR
DREAMS CAN
BE A DARK,
LONELY PLACE.

Obadiah Banana, the ancestor of Banana Joe's family, used a blue fountain pen to sign the registry when he first came to this country.

You can chew your own pen, but don't chew other people's pens.

Mr. Watterson holds the title of the laziest person in all of Elmore.

WHEN WRESTLING AN OLD LADY FOR A FROZEN CHICKEN, DON'T FORGET TO LOOK FOR A DISCOUNTED SALMON, TOO.

When things get a little boring between you and your best friend, you need a third best friend.

BEFORE

AFTER

MOST PEOPLE THINK A BANANA IS A FRUIT, BUT IT IS ALSO CLASSIFIED AS AN HERB.

The most important night of Mr. Robinson's life was spent performing in the Elmore Senior Talent Show.

There were only two acts in the show.

Gumball was a very ugly baby.

WHEN YOU FLOOD YOUR ENTIRE HOUSE,
IT'S HELPFUL IF YOUR BEST FRIEND IS A FISH.

TO PLAY FRUITBALL, YOU NEED TO START WITH THE RIGHT FRUIT. WATERMELON IS ALWAYS A GOOD CHOICE.

When you're feeling like a loser, try looking at this. It'll cheer you right up.

When you're feeling low and need a little cheering up, try looking at this.

GUMBALL'S HERO IS HIS FATHER.

Never call yourself a "pizza delivery guy." Call yourself an "Italian Food Distribution Engineer." It sounds much more impressive (although it's really the same thing).

ROCKY ROBINSON'S FAVORITE ROCK BAND IS AB/CD.

DARWIN DOESN'T BELIEVE IN VIOLENCE. THAT'S BECAUSE HE'S A PACIFISH!

You don't want to mess
with Bobert, especially
when he's in combat mode.

A pink slip means you're fired. That can happen if you show up seven hours and fifty-eight minutes late for your new job.

Everyone would be able to understand Juke if they switched his audio button to VOICE.

VOICE

MUSIC

TO WIN THE FAVORITE TEACHER AWARD, YOU NEED A LETTER OF RECOMMENDATION FROM A STUDENT WHO LIKES YOU.

THAT'S REALLY HARD TO GET WHEN NO STUDENT LIKES YOU.

Banana Joe sings like
a dog with rabies.

It's not
easy being
a piece
of toast,
especially
when
surrounded
by birds.

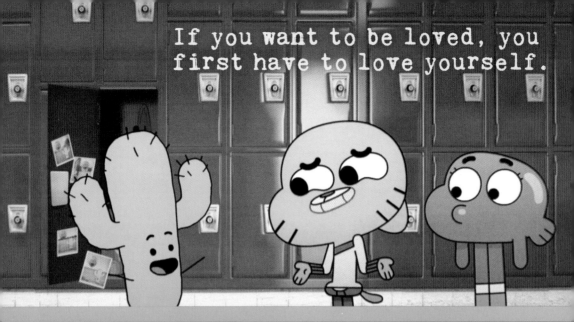

If you want to be loved, you first have to love yourself.

It's easy to tell when Alan is sad.

He deflates.

Monkeys have hair all over their bodies, except for the parts where they need it the most.

WHEN GUMBALL'S DAD GETS A JOB, IT UPSETS THE BALANCE OF THE UNIVERSE.

DAY TURNS INTO NIGHT.
SUMMER TURNS INTO WINTER.

SOMETIMES A NICE, RELAXING MASSAGE IS JUST WHAT YOU NEED DURING A HARD DAY SPENT GROCERY SHOPPING.

The problem with being dumb is that sometimes it really hurts.

Darwin
the First
died under
Gumball's bed.
No one knows
how he got
there.

There is
no point to
cleaning
under the
bed. It's
designed to
be filthy.

Most of all, a best friend should be really good at listening.

VIRUSES CAN BE PARTICULARLY VENGEFUL IF YOU WASH YOUR HANDS

THE DUMP IS THE GREATEST DEPARTMENT STORE IN THE WORLD BECAUSE EVERYTHING IS FREE.

GUMBALL DOESN'T HAVE A HAPPY PLACE.

BUT EVERYWHERE IS DARWIN'S HAPPY PLACE.

CARRIE CAN'T TAKE A SCHOOL PHOTO, BECAUSE SHE'S A GHOST.

GUMBALL'S CELL PHONE WAS MADE B.I. "BEFORE INTERNET."

Hector's hamster died, but he thinks it's hibernating.

Kenneth the microwave monster has quite an appetite.

BUT EVEN MICROWAVE MONSTERS DESERVE A SECOND CHANCE.

Animals protect their territories, whether it's a dog and his yard or Tobias and his school-bus seat.

NACHOS AREN'T FRUIT.

ELMOREPLUS

Store Modify Past Stuff See Aid

ELMOREPLUS

ELMOREPLUS

HOME   MY ACCOUNT   FRIENDS   HELP

GUMBALL&DARWIN

PROFILE PICTURE   - MODIFY

Messages   (0)

PHOTOS

VIDEOS

posted by EggH3aD

EggH3aD

add a comment

I think you'll

SHARE TO

Friends

SEND AN INVITATION

Done

FOR CHRISTMAS, ANAIS WANTS TO GET FOUR PONIES AND TO MARRY A PRINCE WHEN SHE'S OLDER.

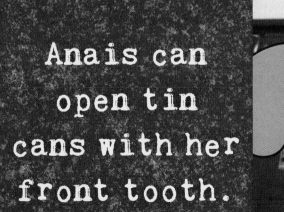

Anais can open tin cans with her front tooth.

SAFETY TIP:
IT'S NEVER A GOOD IDEA
TO STARE DIRECTLY AT
THE SUN.

Gumball's mom works long hours at the Rainbow Factory.

The Reject Club offered to let Gumball join, but he rejected them.

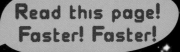

A good mother
prevents accidents
before they happen.

HECTOR WAS PENNY'S DATE TO RACHEL'S PARTY, BUT IT WASN'T A PERFECT MATCH.

A date is a social activity undertaken by two people to determine their suitability for a relationship. It is also a fruit that makes you go.

Armed with Wanda, the Wonderful Wand of Wonder, Mr. Watterson becomes the Mighty Bunny Warlock.

ON ELMORE PLUS, YOU CAN SEE WHAT EVERYBODY IS UP TO AND HOW HAPPY THEY ARE.

IT'S LIKE REAL LIFE, BUT WITH NONE OF THE CONSEQUENCES.

Darwin can't kiss his own tail. He's just not that limber.

Darwin doesn't have hair, because of the stress of everyone being mad at him all the time.

Gumball and Darwin are allowed to babysit Anais because they are very responsible.

Or at least mostly responsible.

Sort of.

Juke comes from the continent of Boomboxemberg.

In Boomboxemberg, they have over five hundred words for disco, and disco is not one of them.

Mrs. Watterson was legally banned from playing patty-cake at the age of seven.

IT'S NOT LITTERING IF YOU PUT GARBAGE IN SOMEONE ELSE'S TRASH CAN.

THE BEST RIDE AT THE FAIRGROUND IS THE STOMACH DESTROYER ROLLER COASTER.

Look inside yourself,
and you'll see how beautiful you are.
Unless you look at today's breakfast.

You wouldn't be naked IF you hadn't thrown away MY lunchbox.
That's still no excuse to eat all MY clothes!
I WAS HUNGRY!

A DVD can look remarkably similar to a pizza cutter.

Gumball has watched the video *Alligators on a Train* seventy-two times.

Friends high-five one another.

Miss Simian has never had friends.
She isn't even sure what friends are.

IDAHO IS A BUMPKIN FROM THE COUNTRY.

HE CAN SHOW YOU HOW TO ATTAIN ULTIMATE HAPPINESS, ASSUMING YOU ARE HAPPY WITHOUT TV, ELECTRICITY, CARS, OR SUPERMARKETS.

TINA CAN'T PLAY
THE PIANO VERY
WELL, BECAUSE
SHE HAS ONLY FOUR
FINGERS, AND THEY
ARE QUITE LARGE.

Darwin has a hard time being direct with people, but Gumball doesn't.

Childhood rule #4: Never take a toy out on the school bus.

Here are three ways to avoid hyperventilating:

1 Breathe through pursed lips (like when you whistle).

2 Slow your breathing.

3 Try belly breathing.

THE LIBRARY MAKES YOU SMART BECAUSE IT'S FILLED WITH BOOKS. BUT YOU CAN'T JUST WATCH A BOOK, YOU HAVE TO READ IT.

You need a big head to be really smart.

THE ROBINSONS LOVE CANNED FOOD, LIKE CANNED YOGURT, CANNED PIZZA, CANNED BUTTER, AND CANNED WATER.

Mr. Watterson's hugs are warm enough to heat a town for eighteen days.

His body is 70 percent sugar.

WHEN YOU WORK FOR FERVIDUS PIZZA,
TEARING APART THE FABRIC OF THE UNIVERSE
IS NOT A DISMISSIBLE OFFENSE.

Molly has a wonderful eye for interior design.

SORRY, GUMBALL AND ANAIS:
DARWIN IS THEIR DAD'S FAVORITE.

BEING A GHOST IS PRETTY AWESOME.

YEAH! WE CAN DO ANYTHING. WE CAN EVEN MAKE A T-REX DANCE.

On Halloween, all ghosts must return to their graves at midnight. No exceptions, and no mortals allowed.

GUMBALL'S MOM IS A LITTLE BIT OF A CONTROL FREAK.

PLASTIC MAGIC WANDS, LIKE WISHBONES, DON'T USUALLY GRANT WISHES.

When Gumball's dad discovered that magic was a fraud, he screamed for fifteen years straight.

A dodeca-dork is a twelve-sided dork. Which shouldn't be confused with a deca-dork, which would be a ten-sided dork.

YOU REALLY, REALLY, REALLY DON'T WANT TO RUN PAST A PACK OF DOGS WHILE WEARING A SUIT OF HAM.

When jealousy takes over your body, it must be expelled.

FIRST, YOU NEED TO CREATE A CIRCLE OF PEPPER.

YOU DON'T WANT TO WAKE A SLEEPING T. REX. THEY CAN BE PRETTY CRANKY.

ESPECIALLY WHEN THE T. REX SLEEPS ON A GIANT MOUND OF SCARY GARBAGE.

Sure, piercing a tube of glue
like a psycho can be sweet revenge.

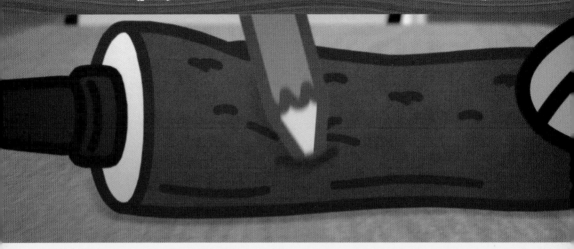

But first, try some herbal infusion tea.
It's very good for the nerves.

ONCE YOU START THE GAME DODJ OR DAAR, IT HAS TO BE FINISHED. OR ELSE.

Sometimes you have to face the consequences of your actions. And other times, you just have to run.

Carrie enjoys being miserable.

SHE CAN TURN HER HEAD AROUND COMPLETELY BECAUSE SHE DOESN'T HAVE BONES.

IT'S EASY TO FALL IN LOVE WITH A BEAUTIFUL GIRL IN A DRESS.

EVEN IF THAT GIRL IS GUMBALL, OR RATHER
GUMBALLOUPSEGGWOBBLEUNDERPANT.

When you cheat,
the only person you're
cheating is yourself.

PRINCIPAL

DARWIN ONLY KNOWS THREE NUMBERS: TWO, *SEVEN*, AND **NINE**.

IT'S NOT A PARTY UNTIL MISS SIMIAN AND MR. BROWN SHOW UP.

Warning: Cry with caution! If you cry too much, all the moisture may leave your body.

Carmen cries dry tears, because cacti don't retain water.

If you're trapped in a bathroom, don't worry. You can always flush yourself out through the toilet.

Any conflict can be resolved with three tools: a mirror, water, and an hourglass.

A MIRROR REMINDS US THAT AN ENEMY IS JUST OURSELF BUT SEEN FROM ANOTHER ANGLE.

WATER REMINDS US THAT WE ALL HAVE SOMETHING IN COMMON.

AN HOURGLASS IS FOR THE TIME WE NEED TO REACH AN UNDERSTANDING.

IF A POTATO PLAYS VIDEO GAMES AND EATS TOO MUCH JUNK FOOD, IT CAN GO INTO TOXIC SHOCK.

When a vegetable gets sick, it doesn't need a doctor— it needs a gardener.

Gumball doesn't want to be just any doctor when he grows up. He wants to be a handsome doctor.

Or maybe a lifeguard.

You should try to channel destructive behavior into something creative, like painting.

I ♥ My Family

MASAMI'S FATHER OWNS THE RAINBOW FACTORY.
IT'S EASY TO TELL WHEN MASAMI IS UPSET, BECAUSE SHE TURNS GRAY AND STORMY.

IF YOU'RE A GHOST, PEOPLE CAN'T SEE YOU. BUT IF YOU WERE BORN A GHOST, THEN EVERYONE CAN.

TO BECOME PART GHOST, TAKE A DROP OF CARRIE'S GHOST POTION. BUT ONLY TAKE ONE DROP.

DO NOT STAND ON THE CUPBOARD DOOR TO REACH COOKIES. INSTEAD, HAVE YOUR BROTHER STAND ON THE CUPBOARD DOOR FOR YOU.

Gumball can't swim.

But Darwin belongs to
a synchronized-swimming club,
along with Penny and Dog.

WITH YOUR OWN SUPER-HIGH-TECH ROBOT, YOU COULD SAVE DOLPHINS, SOLVE GLOBAL WARMING, AND BRING PEACE TO THE WORLD. OR JUST GOOF AROUND.

WHAT IS THIS?

"The valley betwixt two hills.
Its name begins with a b, ends with two t's,
And has u in the middle."

During a total solar eclipse, the moon passes in front of the sun and casts the Earth in darkness.

In ancient times, some people believed a solar eclipse meant the end of the world. We know better now. Or at least, most of us do.

The best way to survive a fight is to wear the Super Bully Protection Suit of Power. It even has tassels.

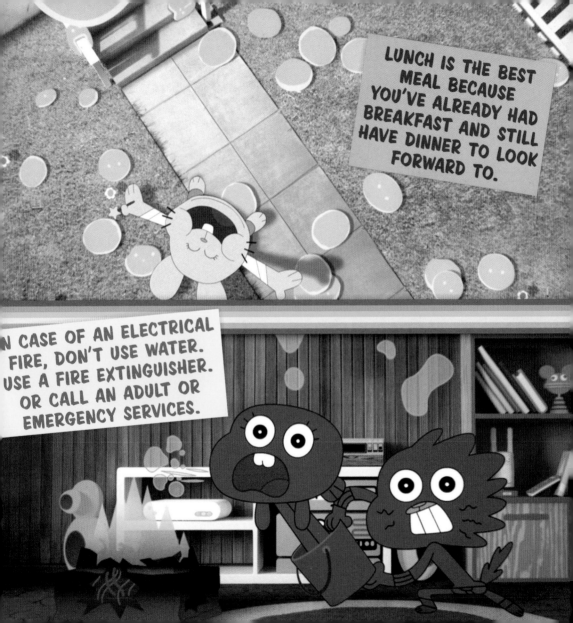

William is Gumball and Darwin's sworn enemy.

WATCH WHAT YOU SAY AROUND HIM. HE'S MISS SIMIAN'S SNITCH.

OCHO

IS AN 8-BIT SPIDER.

Gumball and Darwin didn't destroy Mr. Robinson's new car.

It was a total family effort.

Sometimes, the smallest person in the family is the smartest.

A milk shower is a quick way to get ready in the morning.

MARVIN IS TOO OLD TO DO SIT-UPS.

IT'S HARD TO GUESS WHO WOULD WIN A FIGHT BETWEEN TINA AND BOBERT.

The gross jar is filled with snot, chest hair, sour milk, bird droppings, and other things just as horribly awesome.

The atomic power of the microwave can bring things to life—especially really, really gross things.

GUMBALL'S FAVORITE SWEATER CAME FROM A SEWAGE OUTLET.

A COMPUTER KEYBOARD HAS MORE GERMS THAN A TOILET SEAT.

Teri is a hypochondriac. A hypochondriac is someone who is abnormally worried about his or her health.

Because Gumball and Darwin are kids, they have to do what Mom tells Dad to tell them to do.

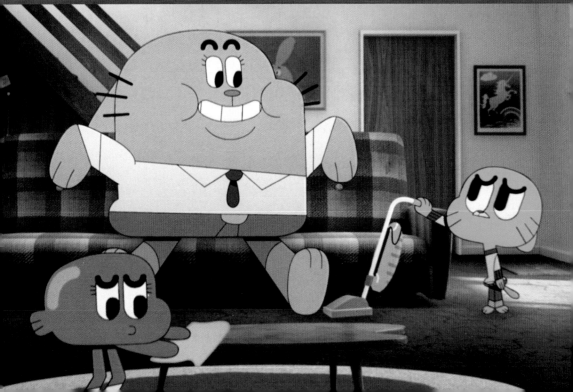

Alan can't roll dice, because he has no hands. He can't play catch, either.

Alan looks good in every photo, even after running a marathon with the flu.

It took **Miss Simian** 754 years to collect all her teaching trophies.

THIS IS HOW YOU DO A SULKY FACE
(IT'S ALL IN THE DETAILS).

When Gumball and Darwin left
Banana Joe behind after a camping
trip, he had to walk home in
the snow and got frostbite,
and that's sort of why
he doesn't have feet.

IT'S NOT A NICE FEELING TO BE AT THE BOTTOM OF THE FOOD CHAIN.

An interpretive dance is a dance in which you channel your emotions through body movements.

PRANKS ARE ONLY FUNNY WHEN THEY HAPPEN TO SOMEONE ELSE.

Ghosts can't eat and so they are usually very hungry.

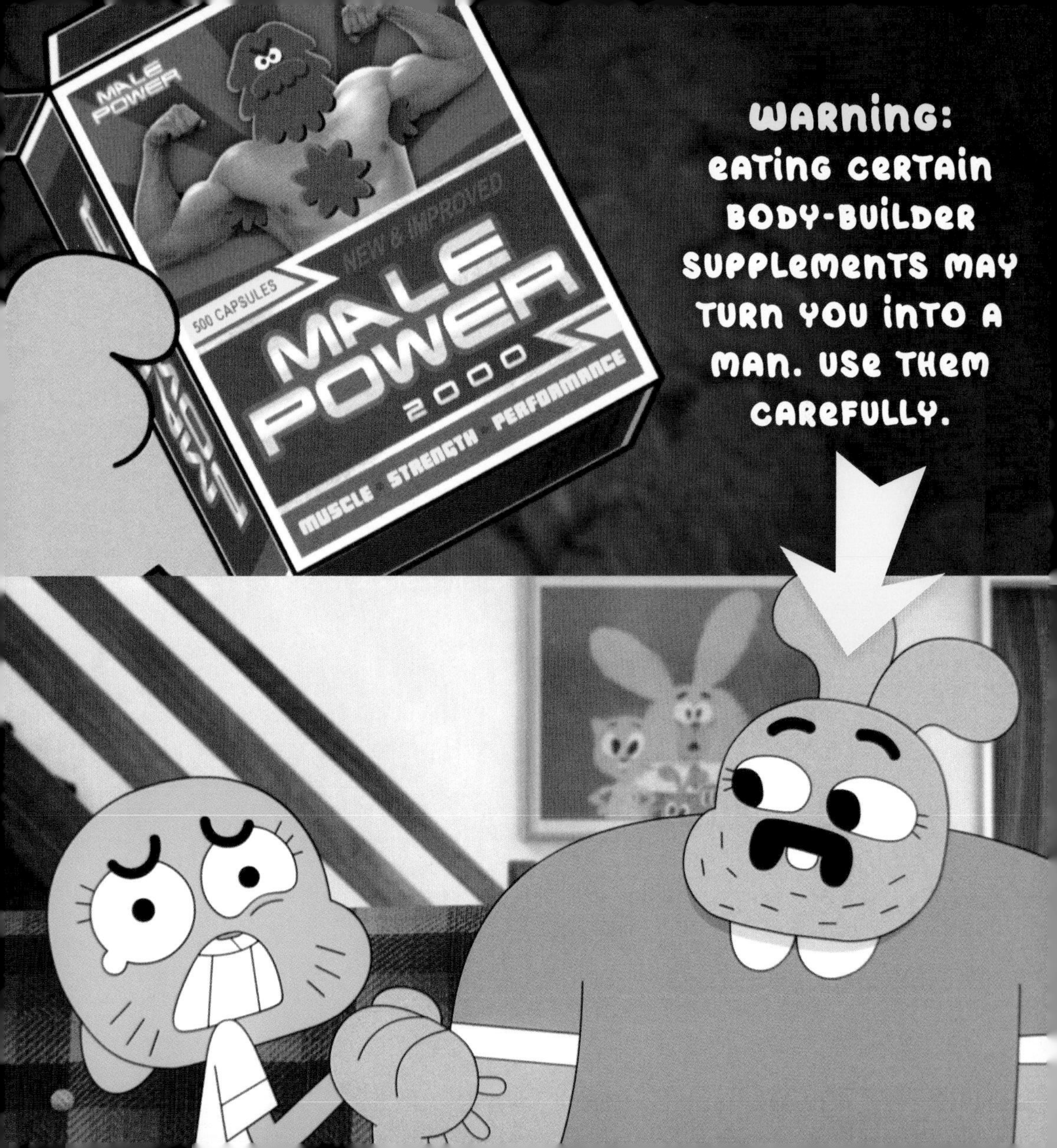
MALE POWER
NEW & IMPROVED
500 CAPSULES
MALE POWER
2000
MUSCLE STRENGTH PERFORMANCE
WARNING:
EATING CERTAIN BODY-BUILDER SUPPLEMENTS MAY TURN YOU INTO A MAN. USE THEM CAREFULLY.

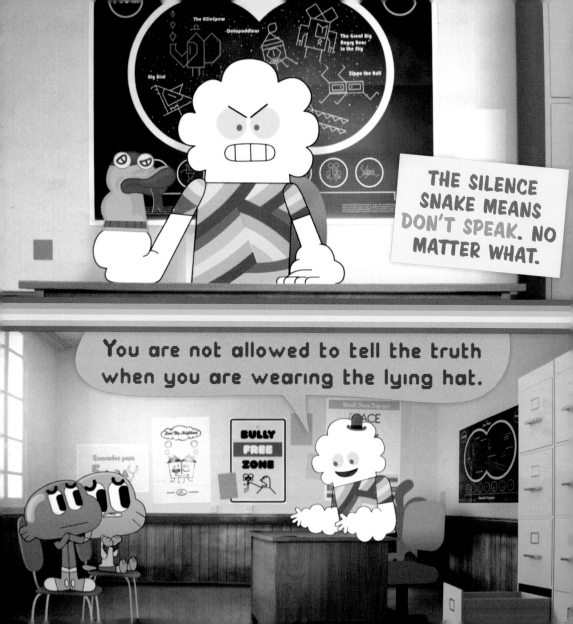

When a student gets **100** percent on an aptitude test, the government has to be alerted.

BRAIN ACADEMY

WARRANT

The Robinsons argue up to six times a day,
sometimes even while they're sleeping.

THE SECRET TO THINKING DUMB
IS TO NOT THINK AT ALL.

INSTEAD OF MILK, CAN WE HAVE CHOCOLATE MILK?
INSTEAD OF EGGS, CAN WE HAVE CHOCOLATE EGGS?
INSTEAD OF THIS BOOK, CAN WE HAVE A CHOCOLATE BOOK?
NO, NO, NO!
Hot Dogs
Hot Dogs

THE ONLY THING SCARIER THAN MESSING WITH A T. REX IS MESSING WITH MRS. WATTERSON.

Anais attends Elmore Junior High School even though she is only four years old.

She's a genius.

But she still sits in a high chair.

When you hang out in the mall with Dad, you can wear your pajamas, eat junk food all day, and get anything you ask for.

IF YOU WANT TO GRAB THE REMOTE, IT HELPS TO BE AN EXPERT IN MARTIAL ARTS.

MR. SMALL IS A LICENSED INLINE SKATER.

Gumball is only about three feet tall.
That means his head is the size of a giant pumpkin.

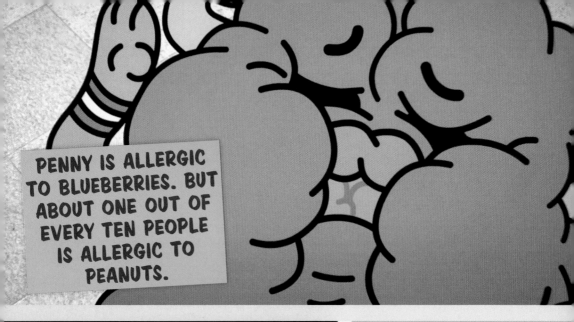

PENNY IS ALLERGIC TO BLUEBERRIES. BUT ABOUT ONE OUT OF EVERY TEN PEOPLE IS ALLERGIC TO PEANUTS.

MORE PEANUTS ARE GROWN IN CHINA THAN ANYWHERE ELSE IN THE WORLD. BUT NONE OF THOSE PEANUTS HAVE ANTLERS.

It's not easy to make a blood pact when you can't draw any blood.

Never mess with Granny Jojo.

A few places you should never ask for free candy: rat-poison factories, abandoned hospitals, dimly lit cellars, but most of all—creepy graveyard houses.

On Halloween all the spirits come out and visit a single desolate house to party.
Mortals are not invited.

HERE'S HOW TO PLAY "I'M THE PRESIDENT"—DO EVERYTHING THE PRESIDENT TELLS YOU TO DO.

EVEN IF HE ORDERS YOU TO FIND THE SMELLIEST THING IN THE HOUSE.

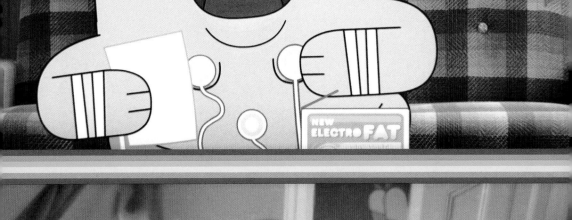

WITH ELECTRO FAT, YOU CAN GET FIT WHILE YOU WATCH TV.

NEW ELECTRO **FAT**

DARWIN CAN HOLD HIS BREATH FOR EIGHTEEN HOURS, FORTY-ONE MINUTES, AND TWELVE SECONDS. BUT THEN AGAIN, HE IS A FISH.

It's nice to get attention from your mother, as long as you don't get too much attention.

Gumball's favorite fruit is Banana Joe.

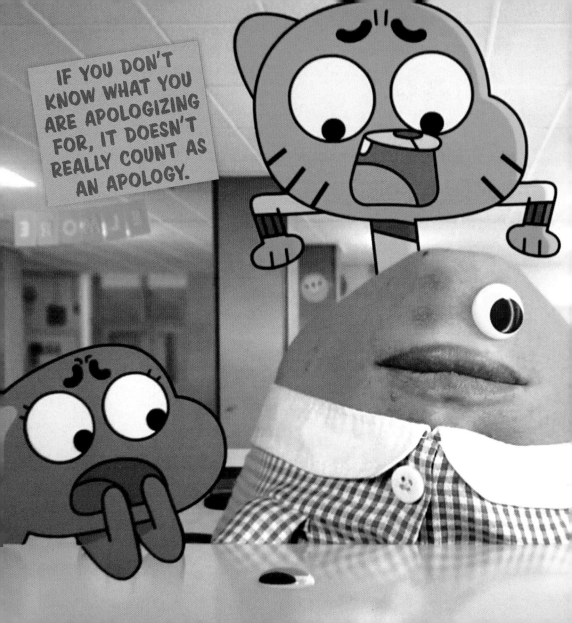

IF YOU THINK AS HARD AS YOU CAN, THEN MAYBE—JUST MAYBE—DAISYLAND TICKETS WILL FALL FROM THE SKY.

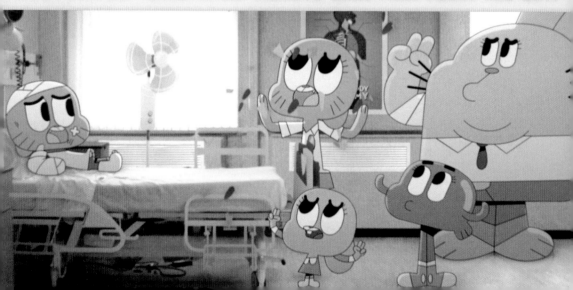

The best thing about failure is that it builds your sense of humor.

FEW THINGS ARE MORE DELIGHTFUL THAN
BATHING IN A TUB OF MELTED CHEESE.

You used up all your good luck in one day, so you're left with nothing but bad luck today.
Is that supposed to make me feel better?

Larry Needlemeyer used to be known as Lazy Larry, but that was years ago.

WANTED

IF YOU WORK AT THE GAS STATION, YOU'RE NEVER ALLOWED TO SLEEP.

Jamie is half cow and half troglodyte. Troglodyte is another word for caveman.

IF THE WORLD IS ABOUT TO END, DON'T HIDE IN AN OUTHOUSE. FOR ONE THING, IT'S CRAMPED. FOR ANOTHER, IT'S JUST A BIG TOILET.

Mr. Watterson's head is so thick he can survive a half a ton of roofing tile and a satellite dish falling on it.

He weighs the same as a car and a half.

CHEATING ON A MATH TEST CAN GET YOU SENT TO THE DETENTION BLOCK.

YOU DEFINITELY WANT TO AVOID THE DETENTION BLOCK.

No matter how far you bug out your eyeballs, you still cannot read someone else's mind.

Mr. Watterson invented a sausage pen.

He also bought a star for his great-great-great-great-great-great-great-grandchildren's children.

IT'S BETTER TO WEAR YOUR MOTHER'S WEDDING DRESS TO SCHOOL THAN TO WEAR NOTHING AT ALL.

Can you keep a secret? Alan gives
all his allowance money to charity.

To get to the picnic area, you don't go through the Forest of Doom. You have to go around the Forest of Doom.

No matter how loud you shout, I still can't break the laws of physics!
Try putting some effort into it.

LESLIE PLAYS THE FLUTE IN THE SCHOOL BAND.

PENNY AND LESLIE ARE COUSINS.

DARWIN ISN'T JUST ANY SORT OF FISH. HE'S A SUCKERFISH.

Anais smells like cinnamon.

Mr. Watterson tries to eat Larry because he thinks he's a hamburger. That sort of thing can happen when you're on anesthetics.

WHEN IDAHO needs TO CHEER UP, HE LiKES TO SiNG SONGS.

CSD stands for Compulsive Singing Disorder.

ELMORE'S SHERIFF LOVES EATING DOUGHNUTS, EVEN THOUGH HE IS A DOUGHNUT HIMSELF.

THE VERY FIRST DOUGHNUT WAS MADE WITH HAZELNUTS AND WALNUTS IN THE MIDDLE OF THE DOUGH, WHICH IS WHY THEY ARE CALLED "DOUGHNUTS."

A broken heart is like a mirror.

It's better to leave it broken than
to hurt yourself trying to fix it.

Gumball is always there for a friend in need, even if that friend is a ghost who wants to possess his body.

THE ONLY SUREFIRE WAY TO DESTROY GUMBALL'S TINFOIL HAT IS TO THROW IT INTO THE GARBAGE CRUSHER AT THE SUMMIT OF MOUNT DUMP.

YOU MIGHT NOT WANT TO KISS DARWIN, BECAUSE HE TASTES LIKE FISH.

DARWIN IS HAPPIEST WHEN HE IS HELPING PEOPLE WHO ARE LESS FORTUNATE.

Freedom is a beautiful thing.
But sometimes you have to say no—
no matter how hard it might be.

When someone saves
your life, the universe
demands that you save his
or her life in return.

If someone joins you when you sleep in
a Dumpster, you might become good friends.

Tobias and Banana Joe are on the football team. But they mostly just hang out in the locker room, even during games.

Unfortunately for him,
Gumball's toothbrush was
actually his dad's back brush.

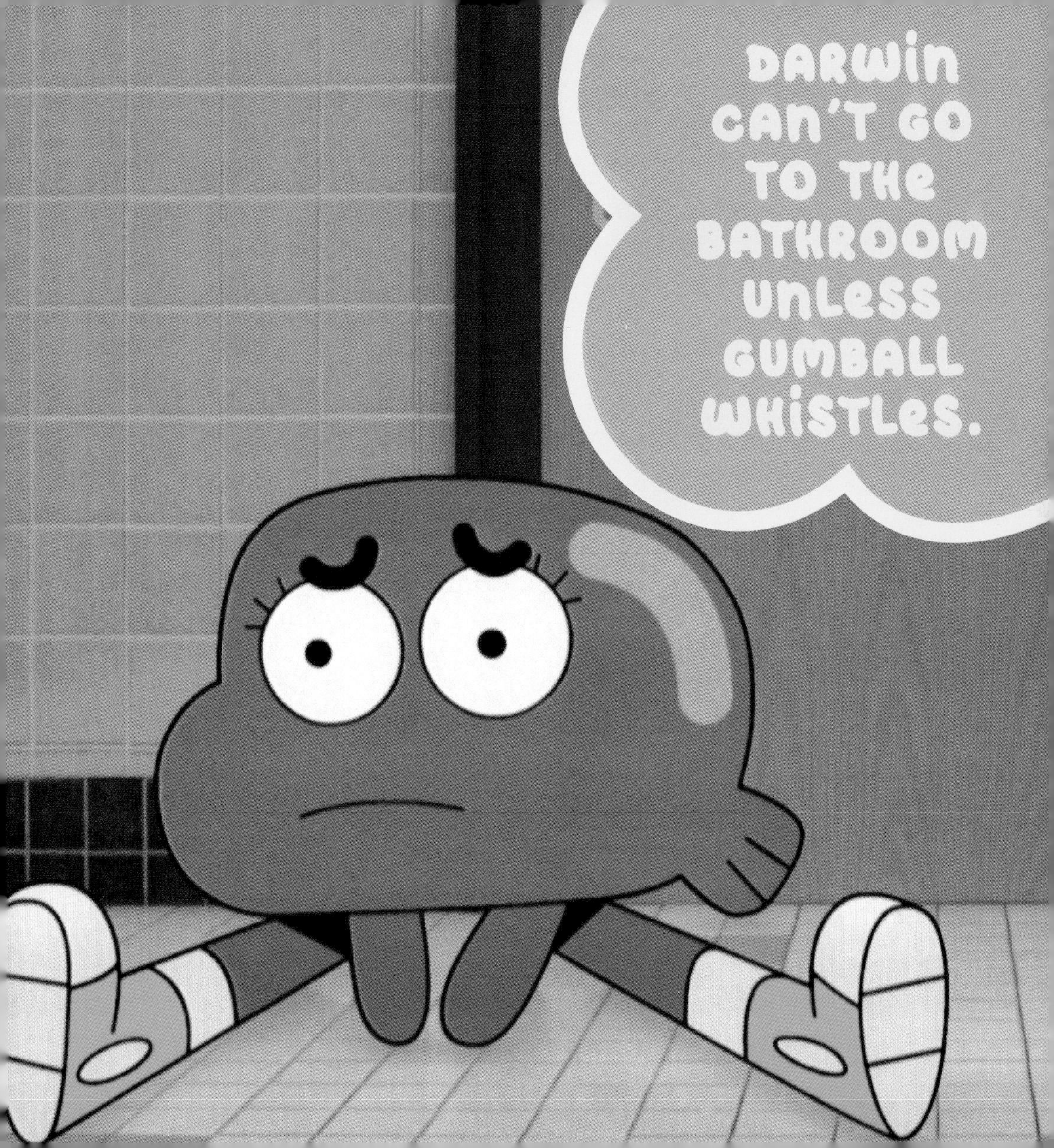
DARWIN CAN'T GO TO THE BATHROOM UNLESS GUMBALL WHISTLES.

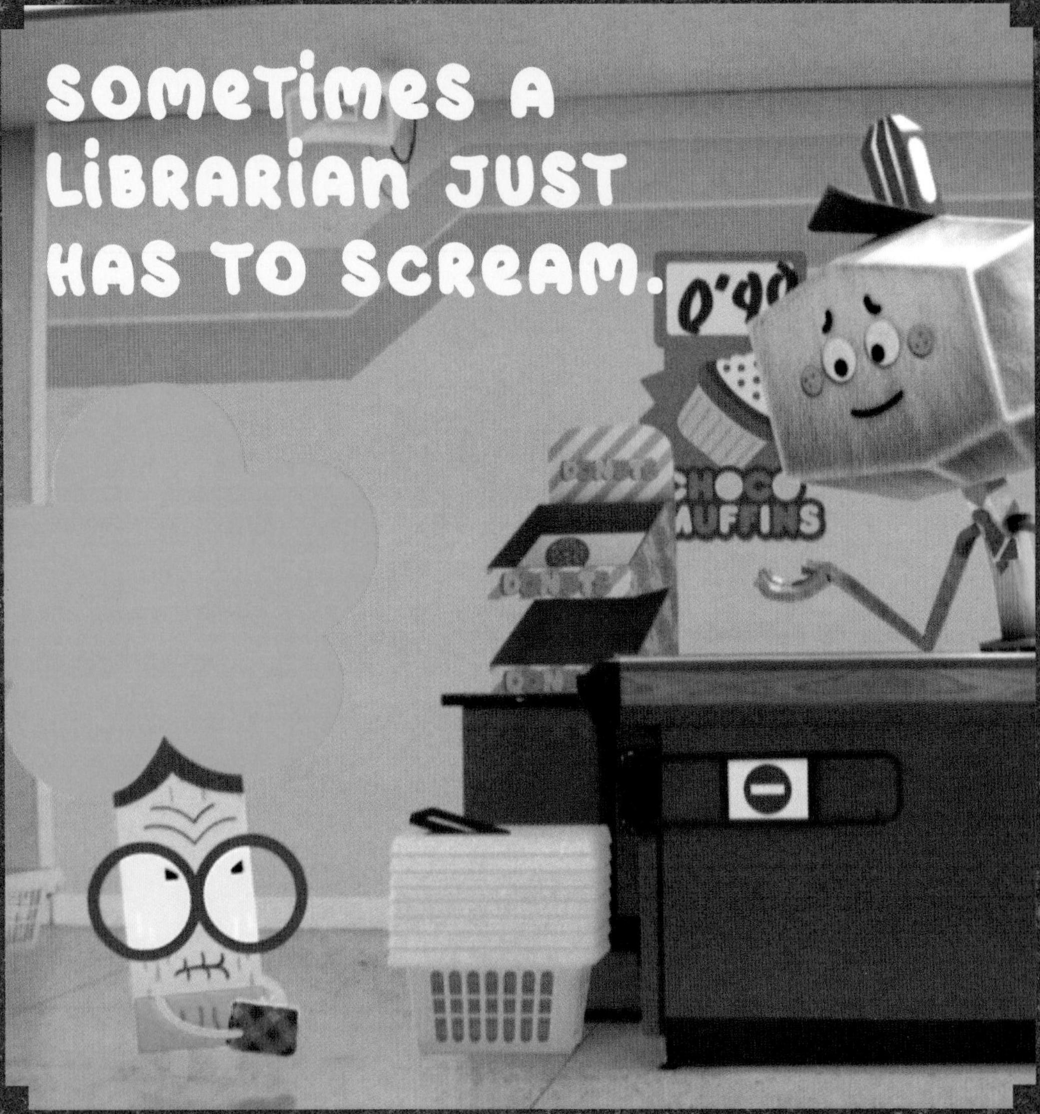
SOMETIMES A LIBRARIAN JUST HAS TO SCREAM.

A handshake is more powerful than a fist.

YOU CAN'T RETURN SHOES AFTER YOU'VE FILLED THEM WITH BAKED BEANS.

When Gumball's father was a kid, he thought he was the Cottontail Cavalier.

A tarantula's bite is no worse than a bee sting
You would need to be bitten about 150 times
before needing to go to the hospital.

Here's one more: What's better, cheese or cake?
I don't know.

Cheese. That's because you can always have cheesecake, but you can't have cakecheese.
That makes sense.

Miss Simian has been teaching for the past three hundred thousand years.

That's a lot of students she's yelled at.

WHEN VIEWED FROM ABOVE, THE FOREST OF DOOM HAS AN UNCANNY RESEMBLANCE TO A SKULL.

All Granny JoJo has to look forward to in her old age are her cop shows and kissing her grandchildren.

But her grandchildren are not looking forward to being kissed by her.